First published in 2013 in the United Kingdom under the title *A Royal Fairytale* by Egmont UK Limited
The Yellow Building, 1 Nicholas Road, London, W11 4AN
Published in the United States of America in June 2013
by Bloomsbury Children's Books
www.bloomsbury.com

For information about permission to reproduce selections from this book, write to
Permissions, Bloomsbury Children's Books, 1385 Broadway, New York, New York 10018
Bloomsbury books may be purchased for business or promotional use. For information on bulk purchases please contact
Macmillan Corporate and Premium Sales Department at specialmarkets@macmillan.com

Library of Congress Cataloging-in-Publication Data
Rivard, Joanna.
A real prince is hard to find : a modern fairy tale / by Joanna Rivard ; illustrated by Adam Larkum. — First U.S. edition.
pages   cm
"First published in Great Britain in 2013 by Egmont UK"—T.p. verso.
ISBN 978-1-61963-215-8 (hardcover) • ISBN 978-1-61963-216-5 (reinforced)
1. William, Prince, Duke of Cambridge, 1982– —Juvenile literature. 2. Catherine, Duchess of Cambridge, 1982– —Juvenile literature.
3. Royal couples—Great Britain—Juvenile literature.
I. Larkum, Adam, illustrator. II. Title.
DA591.A45W55745 2013   941.086'120922—dc23   [B]   2013007772

Art created with a dip pen with Winsor and Newton black ink and Photoshop
Typeset in Napoleone Slab

Printed in the U.S.A. by Phoenix Color Corporation, Hagerstown, Maryland
1 3 5 7 9 10 8 6 4 2 (hardcover)
1 3 5 7 9 10 8 6 4 2 (reinforced)

All papers used by Bloomsbury Publishing, Inc., are natural, recyclable products
made from wood grown in well-managed forests. The manufacturing processes
conform to the environmental regulations of the country of origin.

A Real Prince Is Hard to Find

A Modern Fairy Tale

Kate & William

Joanna Rivard  illustrated by Adam Larkum

BLOOMSBURY

NEW YORK LONDON NEW DELHI SYDNEY

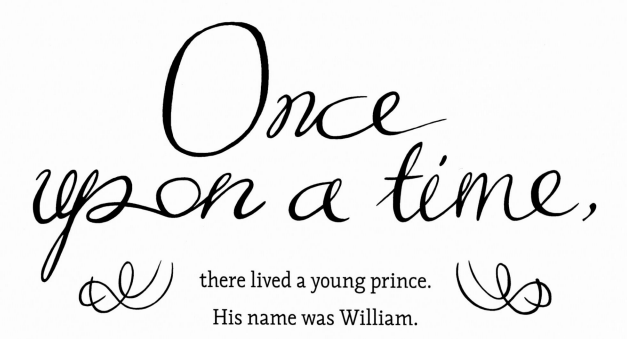

Once upon a time,

there lived a young prince.

His name was William.

He knew that one day he would grow
up to become king.

But he wondered whether he might be lonely in the palace
(it was very large).

Not far from William's palace, in the middle
of the countryside, there lived a young girl.

Her name was Catherine, but everyone called her Kate.

She was terribly pretty.

Like many little girls,
Kate dreamed of meeting
a handsome prince.

But real princes are quite
hard to find.

So when she grew up

she went off to university to learn all kinds of interesting things.

One day, quite by chance, Kate met William at university.

He was ever so nice,
and soon they were the
very best of friends.

Kate and William

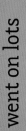

went on lots

of adventures together.

And after they had been friends for a very long time,
William pulled a beautiful ring from his pocket.

"Will you marry me?" he asked.

And Kate said yes!

The whole country was full of excitement.

The royal wedding would be the
event of the year!

Finally the big day arrived.

Just as the clocks struck eleven, Kate arrived at the church.

The wedding went splendidly.
The bride and groom both said "I do" in the right places
(which is the most important part, after all).

And after the wedding,

William's grandmother threw a huge party at her house.

Once the celebrations were over,

William whisked his new bride away to . . .

the Seychelles

Canada

and California

William and Kate were very happy in their new home in the countryside (but it still felt quite large).

There was just one
little thing

they wished for
now . . .

A beautiful baby!

(It's a good thing the palace was
so large after all.)